The Never Girls

in the game

written by
Kiki Thorpe

Illustrated by
Jana Christy

A STEPPING STONE BOOK™

RANDOM HOUSE 🏠 NEW YORK

For Avery and Tessa,

soccer stars and super readers

—K.T.

To my favorite soccer player, Sophia

—J.C.

Copyright © 2016 Disney Enterprises, Inc. All rights reserved. Published in the
United States by Random House Children's Books, a division of Penguin Random
House LLC, 1745 Broadway, New York, NY 10019, and in Canada by Penguin
Random House Canada Limited, Toronto, in conjunction with Disney Enterprises,
Inc. Random House and the colophon are registered trademarks and A Stepping
Stone Book and the colophon are trademarks of
Penguin Random House LLC.

Library of Congress Cataloging-in-Publication Data is available upon request.

ISBN 978-0-7364-3527-7 (trade) — ISBN 978-0-7364-8206-6 (lib. bdg.) —
ISBN 978-0-7364-3528-4 (ebook)

randomhousekids.com/disney

Printed in the United States of America

10 9 8 7 6 5 4 3 2 1

This book has been officially leveled by using the F&P Text Level Gradient™ Leveling System.

Never Land

Far away from the world we know, on the distant seas of dreams, lies an island called Never Land. It is a place full of magic, where mermaids sing, fairies play, and children never grow up. Adventures happen every day, and anything is possible.

There are two ways to reach Never Land. One is to find the island yourself. The other is for it to find you. Finding Never Land on your own takes a lot of luck and a pinch of fairy dust. Even then, you will only find the island if it wants to be found.

Every once in a while, Never Land drifts close to our world . . . so close a fairy's laugh slips through. And every once in an even longer while, Never Land opens its doors to a special few. Believing in magic and fairies from the bottom of your heart can make the extraordinary happen. If you suddenly hear tiny bells or feel a sea breeze where there is no sea, pay careful attention. Never Land may be close by. You could find yourself there in the blink of an eye.

One day, four special girls came to Never Land in just this way. This is their story.

Never Land

Pirate Cove

Torth Mountain

Skull Rock

Pixie Hollow

Mermaid Lagoon

Chapter 1

"Got it!" Kate McCrady yelled.

As the soccer ball sailed through the air, Kate jumped up to meet it. She hovered there, ten feet above the ground, juggling the ball with her feet. She kicked it up, bumped it with her knee, then bounced it off her head.

Some fairies who were flying by stopped to watch. A few clapped.

Kate's friend Mia Vasquez shook her

head and laughed. "Quit showing off, Kate!" she called.

Kate grinned. She couldn't resist one more trick. She leaned way back and booted the ball backward over her head in a bicycle kick.

"Nice one, Kate!" cried her other friend Lainey Winters.

"I've always wanted to do that!" Kate said as she floated gently down. "Why didn't we ever think of playing soccer in Pixie Hollow before?"

"It's fun," Mia agreed. "But I think maybe we put too much fairy dust on the ball." She pointed up at the ball, which was floating like a bubble. It drifted over the treetops and disappeared from view.

"I'll get it!" cried Mia's little sister, Gabby. She jumped into the air. The costume wings she always wore fluttered almost like real fairy wings as she flew after the ball.

Gabby raced into the grove of trees. A second later, they heard a thud and a wail.

"Gabby?" Mia called. "Are you okay?"

"No," came the muffled reply.

"Uh-oh," said Kate. Together with Mia and Lainey, she rose into the air. They found Gabby sitting at the base of a tree. She was holding her nose.

"What happened?"
Mia asked.

"A branch hit me,"
Gabby said.

"Your nose is bleeding!"
Lainey exclaimed.

A few fairies had stopped to see what was wrong. "I'll get a healing-talent fairy!" said the water fairy Silvermist. She darted off toward the Home Tree, the great maple where the fairies of Pixie Hollow lived and worked.

Above her hands, Gabby's eyes looked big and scared. Kate tried to think of something comforting to say. "Don't worry," she told Gabby. "It doesn't look too bad. I've had lots of bloody noses. Yours isn't even a gusher."

Fawn, an animal-talent fairy, gently

stroked Gabby's hair. "There, there," she cooed. "At least your nose isn't important."

"What do you mean?" Gabby asked, looking worried.

"Well, this would be much worse if you were an anteater," Fawn explained. "Or an elephant. They really *need* their noses."

"Fawn!" Mia glared at her. "Your nose is going to be fine," she told Gabby. "It's just a little bump, that's all."

Gabby started to cry. "I want to go home."

"A healing fairy will be here any minute," Lainey reminded her.

"I don't want a healing fairy. I want Mami," Gabby sobbed.

Kate sighed inwardly. If Gabby wanted to leave, then they had go with her. That was the rule they'd all agreed to when they discovered the hole in Mia and Gabby's backyard that led to the magical island of Never Land. They always came and went together. Still, Kate's heart sank a little. After all, they'd only just gotten to Never Land. They still had enough fairy dust to fly all the way to the Mermaid Lagoon and back!

"Come on," Mia said, helping her sister to her feet. "Let's go home."

The girls said good-bye to the fairies and started for the large fig tree that held the portal back to their world. One by one, they ducked into the hollow. They came out behind a loose fence board in Mia and Gabby's backyard. As Kate came through the fence, she had the feeling of stepping into a faded photograph. The sky was a watered-down blue, the grass a dull green.

After the jewel-colored flowers and bright green forests of Never Land, home always seemed plain and drab. Sometimes, Kate thought Never Land seemed even more real than the real world.

As she stood blinking in the harsh sunlight, the back door of the house opened. Mia and Gabby's mother came out. "Kate—" she began, then stopped when she saw Gabby. "*Niña!* What happened?"

"Mami!" Gabby ran into her mother's arms and let herself be cuddled.

"She bumped into a tree," Mia reported. Kate noticed that she carefully left out the part about Never Land. It was the girls' secret. They were the only ones who knew about the hole to the magical world.

Mrs. Vasquez examined her daughter's nose. It had already stopped bleeding.

"You're fine. See? It's just a little bump."

"That's what I told her," Mia said.

"Come inside. Let's get cleaned up." Mrs. Vasquez started to lead Gabby into the house, then turned back. "Oh, Kate, I almost forgot! Your dad just called. He said if you're not home in ten minutes you're going to be late for soccer practice."

"Oh!" Kate exclaimed. The world suddenly seemed to snap into focus. "Thanks, Mrs. V! I'd better go!" She ran for the side gate, calling back over her shoulder. "See you guys tomorrow. Gabby, I hope you feel better!"

"Kate, wait!" Mia said. "Don't forget to—"

Slam! The gate closed behind Kate. She was in such a hurry, she never heard what Mia had been about to say.

Chapter 2

Kate was having her best soccer practice ever. She was the first one to finish the warm-up laps. Then she juggled the ball thirty-three times with her feet without dropping it.

Kate hoped Coach Christy noticed. It was the last practice before the first game of the season, and today the coach was going to assign their positions. Kate wanted to play goalkeeper. She loved being the protector of the net—in the most critical moments of a soccer game, it was all up to the keeper. The few seconds when she was the only thing between an opponent and the goal were the most exciting parts of the game.

But there were at least two other girls who wanted to be goalie. Kate knew the coach might choose one of them. That was why she had to be at the top of her game.

She waited nervously as the coach passed out pinnies and divided the team up for a scrimmage. "Kate, you'll play keeper today," Coach Christy said, handing her a red mesh shirt.

"Yesss!" Kate pumped her fist and ran to stand in front of the goal. She was going to show the coach what she could really do!

The two sides kicked off. For a while,

Kate watched the action eagerly. But as the game wore on, she began to grow impatient. Her teammates were playing great defense. In fact, they'd been so good at keeping the ball away from the goal, Kate had nothing to do! How was Coach going to know to put her in as goalkeeper for the real game if she couldn't see her shine?

"C'mon," Kate whispered, willing the ball to come her way. She braced as the yellow team's striker drove toward the goal. But the red team's sweeper moved in and blocked the shot.

Kate sighed and put her hands on her hips as the ball traveled back down the field. Her mind wandered to Pixie Hollow. *Too bad Coach couldn't see me do that bicycle kick,* she thought. She smiled, imagining the looks on her teammates' faces if she pulled off something like that.

"Kate! Heads up!" Coach Christy shouted.

Kate snapped to attention. The ball was flying toward her and— Oh no! While she'd been daydreaming, she'd moved all the way to the front of the penalty box. She'd left the goal wide open!

Kate leaped into the air, but she knew it was too late. The ball was high over her head. There was no way she could—

Thwump! The ball landed squarely in Kate's arms.

Kate's feet hit the ground and there

was a second of stunned silence. Her teammates stared at her. Kate was just as surprised as they were. *How did I do that?* she wondered.

"Go, Kate!"

"Holy cow!"

"You really flew!"

Flew? Kate thought with a jolt. *Oh no. The fairy dust!* Usually in Never Land she flew until she dropped from the sky and there wasn't a speck of magical dust left on her. But they'd gone home in such a hurry because of Gabby's bloody nose, Kate had forgotten she still had dust on her—until now. She really *had* flown to catch the ball!

Coach clapped her hands. "Okay, Fireballs!" she hollered. "Bring it in."

As Kate jogged over with the rest of the team, she kept her eyes on the ground.

She was afraid to look at her teammates. Could they tell? she wondered. Did they know she had magic? What would happen if the secret of Pixie Hollow got out?

"Nice playing today, everyone," the coach said when the team was gathered around. "Kate . . ."

Kate slowly raised her eyes.

"Incredible save! That's the kind of hustle we need for our game against Westside Thunder on Saturday," Coach Christy said, beaming. "I'm putting you in as goalkeeper."

"I, uh . . . um . . . ," Kate stammered. She knew she should say something about what had happened. But she couldn't find the right words.

The coach seemed to think she was just excited. "It's going to be a tough first game," she told the team. "But I know you've all got what it takes. We're going to have a great season, girls. Now go home and get some rest. See you all on Saturday."

As practice broke up, Kate lingered behind. "Coach Christy," she said, finding her voice. "I'm not sure I can, um . . . make another save like that."

The coach raised her eyebrows. "Why not?"

"Well..." Kate tried to think of a reason that would sound good. "I think that was kind of a one-time thing."

The coach zipped up the red jacket she always wore. "If you can do it once, you can do it again. In all my years of coaching soccer, I've never seen a save like that. You have a natural talent, Kate."

"I wouldn't exactly say *natural*," Kate mumbled.

"The Thunders are a tough team to beat," Coach Christy went on. "We'll need to use every advantage. But I think with you as keeper, we have a really good chance. What do you say?"

Kate hesitated. The coach was counting on her. How could she say no?

"I guess so," she mumbled.

"Don't look so worried," Coach Christy said. "We're going to have a great game."

Kate tried to smile. But she *was* worried. Coach Christy was expecting another amazing save in the game against the Westside Thunders. Kate was good at soccer, but she wasn't *that* good. Her skills alone wouldn't be enough.

There was only one way she was going to be able to play like she had today. She was going to need more fairy dust.

Chapter 3

Faster, Vidia thought. *Faster.*

She zoomed low over the meadow. Blades of grass bowed as she passed, bent by the gust from her wings.

Faster! Vidia blazed over a patch of dandelions, blowing the seeds from their heads.

As she soared again, she spied a swift darting through the air ahead of her. Determined to overtake the swallow-tailed bird, Vidia put on an extra burst of speed.

Faster. Faster. FASTER!

Vidia's wings sliced the air like a pair of knives. Her breath came in gasps. She put every ounce of her strength into passing the bird.

But the swift seemed to sense what she was up to. It sped up, too.

Just when Vidia thought the race might be lost, the wind came up behind her. Vidia smiled. Her old friend, the wind. It gave her just the push she needed. She pulled up alongside the bird.

The swift whistled and swooped away from her.

"Poor thing," Vidia sneered after him. "Afraid you can't beat me?"

Vidia slowed a fraction. She knew chasing the bird would be a waste of time. Swifts weren't good at racing. They were

too flighty to stay on course. Still, she'd been hoping for a good challenge. She looked around for something else to race.

Across the meadow, she spied Dash and Leeta, two other fast fliers. Vidia darted over to them. "Fancy a race?" she asked as she approached them.

Leeta sighed and looked away. "Not today, Vidia."

"Just a quick one. Three times around

the meadow," Vidia wheedled. "That should be a breeze for two fast fliers like you."

"Another time. We're, er, busy," Dash mumbled.

"Very busy," Leeta agreed. With a flutter of wings, the two fast fliers hurried away.

Vidia laughed pityingly at their backs. She knew they weren't busy. They just didn't want to race her. *That's the problem with being the fastest fairy in Pixie Hollow,* Vidia thought. Since she'd already beaten everyone, there was no one left to race.

Vidia scanned the meadow. But all she saw were woolly caterpillars grazing while a fairy herder snoozed nearby. Nothing worth her time. *I'll go and race leaf-boats on Havendish Stream,* Vidia decided. That was always good for a laugh—especially when the sailboats caught the draft from her wings and went swirling off course.

She flew back across the meadow, then followed a gentle slope down past the Home Tree to the fairy docks.

As she passed the mill where the fairy dust was stored, Vidia noticed Kate outside. Kate was talking to Terence, a dust-talent sparrow man. Vidia wasn't usually curious about Clumsies. They were too slow, too awkward, too . . . well, *clumsy.* But she *was* interested in anything to do with fairy dust.

She slowed down to eavesdrop.

". . . just an extra pinch to take home," Kate was saying. "It's for something important."

Terence scratched his head. "Well, we give Peter Pan and the Lost Boys extra

fairy dust to fly," he said. "I suppose there's no harm in you taking a pinch, too."

Terence never gives me *extra fairy dust,* Vidia thought indignantly. When he doled out her daily cupful, he was careful to measure it down to the grain.

Of course, Vidia knew why. More than once, she had helped herself to fairy dust without asking. She had even been banned from going near the mill for a time. But Vidia momentarily forgot all that. She watched, fuming, as Terence scooped a pinch of fairy dust into a leaf. He folded it like an envelope, then sealed it with sap and handed it to Kate.

Kate thanked Terence and put the dust in her pocket. As she walked away, Vidia flew down next to her ear. "Fly with you, sweet."

Kate started and looked around. When she saw Vidia she scowled. "Oh, it's *you.*"

"Is that any way to greet an old friend?" Vidia asked.

"You're not my friend," Kate said. "Friends don't steal all your fairy dust and leave you stuck up in a tree."

"What do you mean, dear one?"

"*You* know," Kate said. "You tricked me into taking fairy dust, when you knew it wasn't okay. Then you took it all for yourself and left me stranded."

"Oh, don't be so touchy," Vidia said, waving her hand. "I seem to recall that you got a rather good flying lesson out of it."

Kate sighed. "What do you want, Vidia?"

"Just what I said, dear child. To fly with you. I thought we might have a race." Vidia's eyes darted to Kate's pocket.

"You can't have any of my fairy dust, if that's what you want," Kate said.

Vidia shrugged as if it made no difference.

"What do you need more dust for anyway?" Kate asked. "You're already the fastest."

In Pixie Hollow, maybe, Vidia thought. But she didn't just want to be the fastest thing in Pixie Hollow. She wanted to be the fastest anywhere, ever. "One can always be faster," she told Kate.

"Well, I don't want to race," Kate replied. "I need the fairy dust for something else." She paused, then added, "Don't you want to know what?"

"Not really," said Vidia. Now that she knew Kate wouldn't race her, she was growing bored with their conversation.

Just as she was about to start away, Kate's friends Mia, Lainey, and Gabby came running down toward the stream. They seemed surprised to see Kate talking to Vidia. "What's going on?" Mia asked.

"Nothing," Kate said quickly.

"Kate, we've been looking for you," Gabby said. "Fawn said the new ducklings are about to hatch. Are you coming to see them?"

"You bet. Bye, Vidia." Kate turned to leave with her friends.

"So long," Vidia said with a shrug, and flew on to Havendish Stream.

Chapter 4

Saturday morning, Kate sat at the kitchen table, pushing her breakfast around on her plate.

"Eat up, Kate," her dad said. "You'll need energy for your game today."

Just looking at her eggs and toast made Kate's throat close up. "I guess I'm not very hungry," she said, setting down her fork.

"Nervous about the game?" her mom asked.

"Mm-hmm." Kate's stomach was tied in

knots. She'd never felt so nervous about a game before. She took a tiny sip of orange juice, then pushed back her chair and stood up from the table. "Can I go over to Mia's?"

"Are you sure that's a good idea?" her mom asked. "Your game is at eleven. You don't want to be late."

Kate glanced at the clock. It was quarter to nine. That left over two hours—more than enough time to see her friends. Kate thought she'd go crazy waiting around at home.

"I won't be late. Mia's house is close to the park. I'll bring my cleats and I can go straight from there to the game," she said.

"All right," her mom agreed. "But don't lose track of the time."

"Thanks, Mom!" Kate ran to her room

to change into her soccer uniform. She put on her jersey and her shin guards. She tied the laces of her cleats together so she could carry them with her.

In the drawer of her desk, Kate found the fairy dust that Terence had given her. *Maybe it's no good anymore,* she thought. *Maybe fairy dust loses its magic after a few days.*

Kate unsealed the leaf and peeked inside. When it caught the light, the fairy dust glittered. It looked as magical as ever.

Kate thought about putting the fairy dust back—just closing the drawer and walking away. Instead, she slipped it into her pocket. She slung her cleats over her shoulder and hurried out of the house, calling, "Bye, Mom and Dad!"

When she got to Mia's, Kate heard her friends' voices coming from the backyard.

As she let herself in through the side gate, a brown-and-white dog came bounding over. It jumped up on her legs.

"Whoa!" Kate cried. "Down, boy!"

"Sorry!" Lainey hurried forward to grab the dog's leash. "This is Rascal. I'm dog-sitting."

Kate raised her eyebrows. "Dog-sitting?"

"You know, like babysitting," Lainey

explained. "My neighbors are out of town and they needed someone to watch him."

Kate knelt down to scratch the dog's floppy ears. "What's wrong with his voice?" she asked. The dog's mouth was opening and closing, but no sound came out.

"I put him in the laundry room last night when we went to bed. He barked all night," Lainey said. "I think he barked himself hoarse."

"Poor guy," Kate said, giving his head an extra scratch. "Can't talk, huh?"

"That's not even the worst of it," Lainey went on. "When I finally let him out so we could get some sleep, he chewed up three pairs of shoes!"

"I believe it," Kate said. Rascal had grabbed the edge of her shorts with his teeth and was playing tug-of-war.

"Cut it out, Rascal," Lainey said, giving his leash a gentle tug. "I can't leave him alone for even a minute. It's a good thing his family is coming home today. My mom won't let him back in the house."

Rascal gave a sudden lunge, jerking the leash out of Lainey's hands. Mia's cat, Bingo, had come creeping around the side of the house. But when he saw Rascal, he turned and ran. Rascal tore after him.

"Rascal! No!" Lainey cried.

In a flash, Bingo was up and over the fence. Rascal threw himself against the slats. His jaw worked furiously, but no sound came out.

"It's like watching TV with the sound turned off," Mia said.

Lainey sighed. "I just have to keep him out of trouble for a little while longer. We thought we'd all take Rascal to the park and watch your soccer game."

"You're coming to my game?" Kate asked sharply.

"Don't you want us to?" Mia asked.

Kate didn't answer. If Mia, Lainey, and Gabby came to her soccer game, they would know about the fairy dust. Not everyone watching would be able to tell she was flying, of course. It wouldn't even occur to most people. But her friends would know for sure.

Kate and her friends had never said they wouldn't fly outside of Never Land. They'd never even talked about it. But she had a feeling they wouldn't like it.

"Hey," Lainey said suddenly, looking around. "Where did Rascal go?"

The yard was empty. "He was just here a second ago," Mia said. "Did you leave the gate open, Kate?"

"No, I'm sure I closed it." Kate ran to check. "See? It's latched."

"Well, then where is he?" Lainey asked.

The girls stared at one another. "You don't think he went to Never Land? Like Bingo?" Gabby whispered. Once, Mia's cat had slipped through the hole in the fence and terrorized the fairies. Just remembering it made Kate shudder.

"But we were standing right here," Mia said. "He probably just wiggled under the fence when we weren't looking. Let's check the front yard."

Outside Mia's house they looked up and down the street. Rascal was nowhere in sight. "I'm the worst dog-sitter ever," Lainey said. "What am I going to tell my neighbors?"

"Don't worry," Kate said. "He can't have gone very far."

"Let's split up to look for him," Mia suggested. "Gabby and I will go up Spruce Street. Lainey, you look on Second Street. Kate, you check the alley. Let's meet back here in a bit."

Kate made her way to the alley behind Mia's house. As she walked along, whistling for the missing dog, Kate's mind went back to her game. She didn't know what to do. If she didn't use the fairy dust, she might be letting her team down. But if she did, she might be letting her friends down. Kate couldn't decide which was worse.

The faint jingle of dog tags interrupted her thoughts.

"Rascal?" Kate scanned the alley but she didn't see him. Was he behind a trash can? "Here, doggy!"

She heard scrabbling overhead and looked up. Rascal was standing on the roof of a nearby garage.

"How did you get up there?" Kate asked in surprise.

Rascal wagged his tail. He looked pleased with himself.

"And how am I going to get you down?" Kate added. She didn't see any easy way onto the roof.

Before she could do anything, Rascal began his silent barking again. He was staring at something in a nearby tree.

"What are you looking at, silly pup?" Kate peered into the branches and saw a squirrel clinging motionless to the trunk.

Rascal began to run toward it, his claws slipping and scratching on the roof's steep shingles. He was headed right for the edge!

"Stop!" Kate screamed as Rascal plunged into the air.

But he didn't fall. He floated! Paws madly paddling the air, he sailed over Kate's head and into the tree.

Chapter 5

For a second, Kate couldn't grasp what had happened. Her first thought was oddly calm. *I wonder if Lainey knows Rascal can fly.*

Then, like the pieces of a jigsaw puzzle snapping into place, it all became clear. "Oh no," Kate whispered. "No, no, no, no."

With a sinking heart, she reached into her pocket. The fairy dust was gone, as she knew it would be. She realized it must have fallen on Rascal when he was tugging at her shorts.

Kate clutched her head. Why had she put the fairy dust in her pocket? She didn't even want to use it!

There was a noise above her and the frightened squirrel suddenly shot from the tree. It leaped onto the roof of the garage. Rascal came right behind. His paws scuttled the air as if he was swimming.

"Rascal!" Kate hissed. "Get down here!"

The dog gave no sign of hearing her. He landed with a thump and tore after the squirrel, his tongue flapping out joyfully.

The terrified squirrel skittered left and right, and Rascal scrambled after it. Together they were making quite a racket.

Kate looked around nervously. Her friends might be here any moment. She didn't want to have to explain how Rascal had ended up in the air.

In desperation, she put her fingers in her mouth and gave a shrill, sharp whistle. *That* got his attention. Rascal stopped and turned. The squirrel took the chance to escape. He darted over the crest of the roof and out of sight.

"Good dog," Kate said. "Good dog." A stick was lying on the ground nearby. Kate picked it up and waved it. "Here, boy! Come get the stick!"

Rascal's ears pricked up. He came a few steps closer. When he reached the edge of the roof, Kate threw the stick, crying, "Go on! Fetch!"

Rascal leaped after it and caught it in midair. As he sailed over her, Kate grabbed the end of the leash that was dangling from his collar. The dog floated above her

like a balloon on a string.

"Good boy, Rascal. Now, bring the stick to me," Kate coaxed.

But Rascal didn't seem to know what to do next. He stared down at her with the stick firmly clenched in his teeth.

"*Good* boy. Bring me the stick," Kate repeated. She gave his leash a gentle tug. Rascal tugged back. He thought it was a game!

Kate suddenly heard the sound of an engine. A car was turning into the alley.

"Rascal! Bring me the stinkin' stick!" she begged.

Out of the corner of her eye, Kate saw a flash of brown fur. Bingo had leaped onto the top of Mia's fence, on the other side of the alley. He crouched there, watching them with a smug expression, as if the whole scene amused him.

When Rascal saw Bingo, he lurched so fast Kate was nearly yanked off her feet. The cat yowled with surprise and leaped back down into Mia's yard. Rascal followed, pulling Kate along with them. She skidded across the alley and slammed into a bunch of garbage cans. The leash slipped from her grasp.

As Kate was picking herself up, the

car rolled to a stop beside her. A woman leaned out the window, peering at Kate through her big sunglasses. "Are you all right?" she asked.

"Yes. I was just . . . uh, looking for something," Kate said.

The woman studied Kate, frowning. "You don't live on this block."

"No. I'm visiting a friend." Kate pointed to Mia's house.

"Well, you shouldn't play back here," the woman said.

"Okay. Sorry." Kate glanced nervously at the sky. She hoped Rascal didn't pick this moment to come flying back.

To her relief, the woman rolled up her window and drove on. As soon as the car turned into a garage, Kate ran over to the Vasquezes' fence.

Bingo was gone. And so was Rascal.

How was she going to find him now? Maybe she could lure Rascal back with dog treats. But where was she going to get those? Or she could catch him with some kind of net! But what net would be big enough?

The more Kate thought about it, the more she realized there was only one way to catch a flying dog. She was going to need more fairy dust.

The way to Never Land lay behind a loose board halfway down the fence in Mia's backyard. Kate hurried there now, hoping her friends hadn't returned yet. She didn't want to have to explain to them why she'd brought fairy dust home in the first place.

She was in luck. The backyard was empty. Kate found the loose board and pushed it aside.

A familiar warm, sweet-smelling breeze blew against her face. Never Land was there, waiting. She knew she could squeeze through the hole, get more fairy dust from Terence, and be back before anyone knew she was gone.

But Kate hesitated. If she went to Never Land now, without her friends, she'd be breaking their promise to always go together.

Kate stood with her hand pressed against the board, her heart pounding. What should she do?

Chapter 6

Vidia was bored. She had already circled Pixie Hollow six times, chased an eagle, and blown all the petals off a blossoming cherry tree. And it wasn't even noon.

She flew around again, looking for something to do. Drowsy bumblebees buzzed in the lavender. Plump caterpillars inched through the grass, herded by yawning fairies. A mouse cart trundled along a path, carrying a heavy load of ripe strawberries. Everything in Pixie Hollow seemed sleepy and slow. It was enough to drive a fast flier crazy!

As Vidia flew past the Home Tree, she saw laundry-talent fairies hanging their wash out to dry. The sight of the sagging, wet linens was too much for Vidia. She started toward them, picking up speed as she flew.

Faster. Faster. Faster.

Vidia zoomed past the laundry, blowing it right off the line. For an instant, sheets and flower-petal dresses swirled through the air.

A second later, they had all landed in the dirt.

"Vidia!" the laundry fairies shrieked.

"What?" Vidia said with a knowing smile. "I was only doing my best to dry

them. Just lending a helping wing, loves. It's not my fault if you didn't pin them tightly."

But the laundry fairies weren't fooled. "A helping wing?" one of them scoffed. "You're just trying to stir up trouble. I swear, you're the most useless fairy that ever was!"

Useless! Vidia felt as if she'd been slapped.

How dare she! She was the fastest fairy in Pixie Hollow!

Well! Vidia didn't need to hang around listening to insults. *Let them get back to their silly washing,* she thought. With a toss of her hair, she flew away.

But with each beat of her wings, the word seemed to echo in her ears. *Useless. Useless.*

Of course, she knew the laundry fairy was wrong. Fast fliers were among the most important fairies in Pixie Hollow. They stirred the breezes that spread pollen from flower to flower and tree to tree. True, Vidia rarely bothered with pollen herself. But that was only because she was too busy training and racing, always pushing herself to be faster. Wasn't being the best enough in itself?

As she passed the fairy dust mill, Vidia thought suddenly of Kate. For the first time, she wondered why Kate had needed the fairy dust. *It's for something important.* That was what the girl had said.

"A race. That must be it," Vidia mused. To her, it was the only reason to need extra fairy dust.

Vidia looked across Havendish Stream to the tree that held the portal. The Clumsy world was usually of little interest to her. She had passed the portal a dozen times that day without a thought. But now she paused to consider. If she wanted to be the fastest flier ever, why shouldn't she go? There would be more things to race—*and to beat,* Vidia thought. Why was she wasting her time in boring old Pixie Hollow, when there was a new world to conquer?

Vidia reached the portal in seconds. The tree hollow was barely big enough for the girls to fit through, but to a fairy it was as big as a cave. For a few seconds, Vidia flew blindly through darkness. She came out blinking in the sudden light, and nearly ran headlong into Kate.

"Vidia!" Kate exclaimed. "What are you doing here?"

"Just paying a friendly visit," Vidia said. "Did you win your race?"

Kate looked confused. "What race?"

Vidia sighed. Really, Clumsies were so slow! "*Your* race, dear child. The one you needed fairy dust for."

"It wasn't . . . I mean, I didn't . . . well, I lost it."

"The race?" Vidia asked.

"The fairy dust!" Kate cried. "And now

I have a big, big problem, and I need more fairy dust to fix it."

Vidia didn't care about Clumsy problems. "Then why don't you scurry off to Terence and ask for some? He seems happy to give you whatever you like," she said sourly.

"But then I'd be breaking a promise to . . . Oh, never mind. I don't expect you to understand. I don't suppose you'd give me any of *your* fairy dust?" Kate added, without much hope. "I wouldn't ask, but it's an emergency."

"You want *my* dust?" Vidia almost laughed. The idea of sharing her dust with anyone was absurd.

But as she thought about it, Vidia realized it was her chance to get exactly what she wanted—*and* prove the laundry

fairy wrong. "I'll help you . . . ," she told
Kate.

Kate's whole face lit up. "Oh, thank
you—"

"On one condition," Vidia added.

"I should've guessed," Kate said with a
sigh.

"I think you'll enjoy it. You're such a
talented flier," Vidia said. "I want a race."

Kate blinked. "Why do you want to
race *me*?"

"For fun, dear child."

"But we both know you'll win," Kate
said. "What's the fun in that?"

That was exactly why it was fun, but
Vidia didn't say so. She wanted Kate to
think she stood a chance—races were
better that way. "Oh, I'm not so sure,"
she lied.

"Fine. I'll race you as soon as we get back to Pixie Hollow."

"No," said Vidia. "Now."

"But I can't right now!" Kate said.

Vidia shrugged. "No race, no dust, darling. What will it be?"

Vidia could practically see the wheels turning in Kate's mind. "All right," Kate agreed finally. "One race. But I'll still need some fairy dust to fly. Otherwise, it won't be fair. Right?"

"Of course." Vidia fluttered over to Kate. When she was above the girl's head, she buzzed her wings, like a hummingbird— once, twice. A small cloud of fairy dust drifted down onto Kate. Vidia was careful to give her only a little. She kept most of it for herself.

"Where should we race?" Kate asked.

"Your choice, love." Now that she'd gotten her way, Vidia was feeling generous.

They both looked around. Vidia knew from her last trip through the portal that they were in Mia and Gabby's backyard. It looked different now, though. Last time there had been snow on the ground.

Kate pointed to a gap between two houses. Far in the distance, Vidia could see a tall pole with a line attached. "We'll race to that telephone pole. Ready?"

Vidia nodded. "Start us off."

"On your mark," Kate said, crouching beside her. "Get set. . . . Go!"

Chapter 7

When Kate said "Go!" Vidia shot forward so fast that Kate could feel the breeze from her wings. In seconds the fairy was far ahead. She looked like a tiny dot of light, a faint shooting star against the blue sky.

Kate watched as she disappeared from view. "Sorry, Vidia," she said softly. "I'll have to race you some other time."

She wondered how long it would take the fairy to notice she hadn't followed.

Kate knew Vidia would be furious at the trick. But right now she had something more important to worry about—finding Rascal.

"Here, Rascal! Here, doggy!" Kate called as she ran back to the spot where she'd left him. She thought she heard the jingle of dog tags. But it turned out only to be wind chimes tinkling in someone's backyard.

She checked up and down the alley, trying to ignore the rising feeling of panic. How long had she been talking to Vidia? Five minutes? Ten? Rascal could be far away by now. And there was no telling which way he'd gone.

Or was there? After all, she had fairy dust. Kate knew from her flights around Never Land that the best way to see in every direction was to look from above.

Kate looked around. The alley was empty. Now was her chance.

She closed her eyes and tried to think light, happy thoughts. She imagined herself floating up like a feather on the breeze. A second later she felt her feet rising off the ground.

Kate opened her eyes and gasped. How different it was flying above her neighborhood! She could see *everything*! She looked straight down into Mia's backyard—there were some toys Gabby had left out on the lawn. And there, two doors down, was Lainey's house, with the old toolshed in the back. *I'll bet I can even see my house from here,* Kate thought, turning to look.

"Oh no!" she whispered. Mia, Lainey,

and Gabby were coming down the block!

Quickly, she ducked behind the branches of a tree. She watched through the leaves as her friends came through the side gate into Mia's backyard.

"Kate? Are you here?" Mia said, looking around. "I guess she's not back yet."

"I can't believe we didn't find Rascal," Lainey said. "What am I going to do?"

"We could put up posters," Gabby suggested. "You know, with a picture of Rascal. Maybe someone will call if they see him."

"I don't have a picture of Rascal," Lainey said. "Besides, I don't want the whole neighborhood to know I lost him. Not yet, anyway."

"Okay," said Mia. "We'll keep looking."

Kate felt terrible. *Poor Lainey,* she

thought. *She thinks it's her fault.* Kate had to find that dog!

She flew up to the nearest rooftop, landed lightly, and looked around.

Mia's street was mostly houses. But on the next block over was a row of tall brick buildings. There Kate saw something strange. A flock of pigeons filled the sky, flapping their wings and cooing. They settled down on a rooftop, only to rise into the air again a second later.

Something is scaring them, Kate thought. And she thought she might know what.

Sure enough, Rascal appeared, soaring through the air like super-dog. He sailed over a gap between two buildings, joyfully chasing the pigeons from their roosts.

Kate flew down the street, leaping

across rooftops and ducking behind chimneys like a spy. But when she reached the block with the tall buildings, she paused. To get to Rascal, she had to cross over a street. Out in the open, someone might see her. There would be nothing to hide behind.

Kate waited as a few cars passed, their drivers hidden inside. On the sidewalk, a woman was pushing a baby stroller.

But her back was to Kate. There was no one else on the block. It was now or never.

Kate took a deep breath and leaped from the rooftop. As she flew across the street, her shadow passed right over the woman in the stroller.

Kate sucked in her breath. Oh no! Her shadow! Why hadn't she thought of that?

The woman stopped, startled. She turned to look up at the sky just as Kate flew over the ledge of the apartment building and quickly ducked down behind it. Safe!

On the far side of the roof, Rascal was still having the time of his life chasing pigeons. But the next time he came flying past, Kate was ready. She grabbed the end of his leash.

Rascal didn't want to be caught. He strained after the pigeons. He was surprisingly strong for such a small dog, even when floating in the air. But this time Kate wasn't going to let him go.

"You're coming with me," Kate said, dragging him toward the edge of the building.

Kate pulled one way. Rascal pulled the other. High in the air, they played tug-of-war. But little by little, Kate was winning. She managed to pull him toward the alley behind the building.

They were almost to the ground when the hairs on Kate's neck prickled. She sensed, even before she saw, that someone else had come into the alley.

Slowly she turned her eyes to the ground. Three astonished faces stared up at her.

"Kate?" Lainey said. "What are you doing?"

Kate didn't know what to say. Her

mouth opened and closed silently. She felt just like Rascal trying to bark.

As if he sensed her hesitation, the dog gave an extra-hard lunge and jerked the leash from her hands. "No!" Kate yelled as he flew up and away.

She was about to go after him. But Mia grabbed her foot. "Kate, get down here! Someone will see!" she hissed.

"I just had him!" Kate groaned as she watched Rascal soar away over the top of the building. But she landed next to her friends.

As soon as Kate was on the ground, they began asking questions all at once.

"What is going on?"

"Where have you been?"

"Why do you have fairy dust?"

"How come Rascal is flying?"

Busted, Kate thought with a sigh. She told her friends how Rascal had accidentally gotten covered in fairy dust, and how she'd tricked Vidia into sharing some of her own so she could go after him.

"But why did you have fairy dust in your pocket to begin with?" Lainey asked.

Kate felt her cheeks grow warm. "For the soccer game," she admitted.

Gabby's mouth fell open. "You were going to *cheat*?"

"No! It wasn't cheating. I was just . . ." Kate trailed off. *It* would *be cheating, wouldn't it?* said a voice inside her. That was why it had felt so bad all along.

That settles it, she decided. *I'm not a cheater, and I never will be.*

"I'm not going to do it," she told her

friends. "It was just a big, big mistake." As soon as she said it, Kate felt better than she had all morning. She turned to Lainey. "I'm really sorry about Rascal. But I'm going to get him back, I promise."

"Okay. But where did he go?" Lainey asked.

"Well, he likes chasing birds and squirrels," Kate said. "So I bet he'll be wherever they are."

The girls looked at each other. "City Park!" they said in unison.

It was three blocks to the park, and they ran the whole way. But when they got there, Kate's heart sank. There were so many people. Even if they found Rascal, how would they get him down without anyone noticing?

"What are we going to do when we find him?" Lainey asked as if reading her thoughts.

"I don't know," Kate admitted. "But the good thing is, he's been flying so much, his fairy dust should wear off soon."

They walked past joggers, bikers, and children playing. There were plenty of dogs in the park, too. But none of them were flying.

As they passed a woman talking to a policeman, Kate overheard the officer say, "A bear? Are you sure, ma'am?"

"Yes," the woman said firmly. "It was a bear, I'm telling you. It was up in a tree."

Kate stopped in her tracks. Her friends stopped, too. "What?" Lainey asked.

Kate motioned to her to be quiet. She knelt and pretended to tie her shoelace so she could listen.

"My son saw it first," the woman was saying. She turned to the little boy standing next to her. "Tell the policeman what you saw, Wade."

"He was up in a tree," the boy said. "He had white spots."

 The policeman frowned. "I've never heard of a bear with white spots. Are you sure it wasn't something else? A raccoon, maybe?"

"It looked like a dog," the boy said.

"I told you, sweetie. Dogs can't climb way up in trees," said his mother. "Are you going to do something about it?" she asked the policeman.

"I'll check it out," he replied. "Where did you say it was?"

"Over there, in those trees." The woman pointed to a leafy section of the park.

Kate straightened up. "C'mon!" she whispered to her friends. "We have to find Rascal before that policeman does!"

They ran as fast as they could. When they got to the trees, they spread out, whistling and calling in loud whispers. "Rascal! Here, boy!"

"I found him!" Gabby yelled suddenly.

They turned to where she was standing. Looking up, Kate saw Rascal sitting high up in the branches of a big tree. He grinned down at her, panting.

"Why is he just sitting there?" Mia asked.

"It looks like his leash is wrapped around the trunk," Lainey said. "Kate, can you get it?"

"No problem."

But just as Kate was about to fly into the branches, Mia grabbed her. "Hello, Officer," she said loudly, squeezing Kate's arm.

Kate turned and saw the policeman walking toward them. "You kids better go play somewhere else," he told them. "I've had a report of a wild animal around here."

"We haven't seen anything, and we've been here all, uh, morning," Mia said, squeezing Kate's arm even harder. Kate knew how much Mia hated to fib.

"No?" The policeman glanced around. *Please don't look up,* Kate silently begged. For the first time, she was glad that Rascal couldn't bark.

The policeman nodded. "Well, let me know if you do. How was the game?" he added, looking at Kate.

"What?" Kate asked, confused.

"How was your soccer game? Did you win?" he asked, pointing to her Fireballs jersey.

Kate clapped a hand over her mouth. She'd almost forgotten about the game! "What time is it?" she asked the policeman.

He looked at his watch. "Eleven on the dot."

"I've got to go!" Kate started to run toward the soccer fields.

"Kate, wait!" Lainey called after her. "What should we do?"

"Don't do anything!" Kate yelled. "I'll fix everything just as soon as I'm back." *I should still have enough fairy dust by then,* she added to herself. But then her stomach dropped.

Oh no! The game was about to start—and she was covered in fairy dust!

Chapter 8

Vidia blazed over the city. She flew past metal chimneys belching steam. She crossed busy roads that roared like raging streams. She passed buildings ten times taller than the Home Tree, each window as big as a cave.

Everything in the Clumsy world was enormous, but Vidia felt far from tiny. Speed made her powerful. She might have been as small as a hummingbird, but she felt like a giant inside.

All through the race, Vidia had been tempted to look back to see how far ahead she was. Instead, she kept her eyes fixed on the finish line. Vidia prided herself on focus. It was what made her better than other fliers.

As the telephone pole loomed in front of her, Vidia put on an extra burst of speed. She shot past the pole, crying, "I win!"

She turned to see Kate's reaction. But Kate wasn't there.

Vidia chuckled. "I flew even faster than I thought!" Of course, she'd known all along that she would win. Still, she was surprised at how far Kate had fallen behind.

She waited, circling the telephone pole impatiently. But as the minutes passed, Vidia realized that Kate wasn't coming.

Somewhere along the way, the girl had dropped out of the race.

"That cheat!" Vidia fumed. "To think I gave her even a speck of my fairy dust!" She started back, plotting what she'd do to Kate when she found her.

But Vidia had been so focused on winning, she hadn't paid attention to what way she'd come. The city roared around her, a confusing maze of buildings and car-clogged roads. Vidia spun in the air.

Then, below on the sidewalk, she spied a flash of long red hair. "Aha!" Vidia snarled. "There you are!"

She made a beeline for the girl, dive-bombing so fast that the air whistled around her. When she reached Kate, Vidia pinched her just above the elbow. Hard.

The girl yelped in surprise. But as she

turned to examine her arm, Vidia saw that it wasn't Kate after all. This girl was much older, almost a grown-up. She looked right at Vidia without seeing her.

Vidia backed away and scanned the crowded sidewalk. *Whoosh!* A bicycle whizzed past, blowing her right out of the air. She landed in the street.

As she picked herself up, the ground began to tremble. She looked up and saw a great metal monster rushing toward her.

For the first time in her life, Vidia froze.

The car passed over her. For a moment, the noise and rumble and fumes seemed to swallow her. Then, an instant later it was gone, and she was coughing on the other side. Vidia breathed a sigh of relief—until she saw the next car coming.

She darted away just in time. She dodged the wheels of another passing bicycle and zipped between the moving legs of people hurrying this way and that. Vidia was nimble and fast, but the city swirled around her, big and confusing.

As far from giant as she'd been when she was racing, now Vidia felt helpless as a bug. She had to get away from this busy street!

When she saw trees, she flew toward them. Vidia recognized the park when she got there. She'd been there once before, with Kate and her friends. Back then it had been covered in snow. It looked different now, with leaves on the trees and the grass all green.

And everywhere she looked she saw Clumsies. Clumsies walking, Clumsies running, Clumsies playing. To Vidia they all looked the same—big, slow, and clumsy.

Then, to her surprise, she spied three Clumsies she actually knew. Mia, Lainey, and Gabby were standing beneath a tree, looking up at something in its branches. Vidia zoomed toward them. They would know where Kate was.

But as she got closer, Vidia slowed, then paused. There was an animal in the tree.

It was smaller than a wolf, but bigger than a fox.

A dog, Vidia thought as the word came to her. Well, that was nothing to worry about. Dogs were dull, earthbound animals, not much better than their Clumsy masters. It was odd, though—she'd never seen one in a tree before.

When it saw Vidia, the dog went into a silent frenzy. But it didn't move from its branch. She looked closer and saw that it was attached to the tree by a tether.

Feeling reassured, Vidia started toward the girls again, flying at her usual high speed. As she dove toward them, she heard a *snap.*

The dog had broken free from his collar. He was running toward her.

No, not running—flying!

As the animal bore down on her, all she saw was its great pink tongue and sharp white teeth. "Rascal, no!" she heard Lainey cry.

Vidia fled. But when she chanced a look back over her shoulder, she saw that the dog was right behind her. Vidia put on a burst of speed.

Then Vidia swerved around a tree. She zigzagged left, right, and left again. But no matter what direction she went in, the dog matched her speed.

Faster. Faster. Faster!

Vidia's shoulders ached. Her lungs were bursting. But the dog showed no sign of stopping. She zoomed on across the park.

She was finally getting the race she had wanted. And it was terrifying!

Chapter 9

On the soccer field, Kate was having her own problems. She stood in front of the goal. Her feet were spread wide. Her hands were ready. Sweat beaded on her forehead.

"I will not fly," Kate whispered to herself. "I will not fly."

The key to flying was to think of light, happy things. Thoughts that made your insides feel like a helium-filled balloon. So Kate tried to do the opposite. She thought of heavy, dreary things—a bad head cold, a backpack full of homework, a birthday party spoiled by rain. She imagined that her shoes were full of wet sand.

Most of all, she imagined losing the game. Unfortunately, that wasn't so hard to do.

"Come on, goalie! Move your feet!" someone's dad yelled as the ball flew past Kate into the net.

Kate's cheeks burned. She hated it when parents yelled at the players. But one glance at Coach Christy told her the dad wasn't too far off. The coach's arms were folded and she was frowning.

There was no doubt about it. Kate was playing her worst game ever. She had promised herself she wouldn't cheat. But that was turning out to be harder than she'd thought. With fairy dust, one little leap could send her soaring. Kate was afraid to do more than shuffle her feet a little.

The teams returned to the midfield line for the kickoff. Right away, the Thunders got control of the ball and brought it back up the field. This time the shot came high and to the right. Kate timidly stretched out her arm to block it. But she didn't even come close. It was only luck that saved her this time—the ball bounced off the goalpost.

The other team had started to catch on, though. Each time they shot, they tried to send the ball high, knowing Kate wouldn't jump for it. At halftime, Kate's team was down 0-2.

"What is going on, Kate?" Coach asked as the Fireballs gulped water. "You look like your cleats are made of lead!"

"Sorry," Kate mumbled into her cup. "I guess I'm just not having a good game."

Coach Christy gave her a long look. Kate was sure she was going to take her out.

For a second, she felt almost relieved.

"Do you like soccer?" Coach Christy asked.

"Yeah," Kate said, surprised. "I love it."

"Then play like you do," the coach said. "Don't worry about what other people think. Just play like it's fun. I know you can do it."

Did I have it all wrong? Kate wondered as she ran back out to the field. She'd thought Coach Christy had only made her a goalie because of her hotshot moves. She'd thought she needed fairy dust to be a good player. But it had only made her worse. She didn't have to cheat—but maybe she didn't have to try so hard *not* to cheat, either.

Maybe Coach Christy was right. Maybe she could just have fun.

Once Kate relaxed, she started to play much better. Her teammates were playing better, too. They scored two goals. Now the teams were tied.

It was the end of second half when the Fireballs' sweeper fouled. The Thunders were awarded a penalty kick.

Kate braced herself as the Thunder's kicker lined up for the shot. This was the moment she'd wanted—and dreaded. It was all up to her. She was so focused, she hardly noticed someone shouting off the field . . . until she heard a familiar name.

"Stop, Rascal! Stop!"

Rascal? Kate looked toward the sidelines and her heart skipped a beat. Rascal was bounding toward the soccer field, right on the heels of Vidia. The dog's fairy dust

seemed to be wearing off—he was leaping rather than flying. But it didn't slow him down any. In fact, every time he rocketed off the ground, he seemed to go faster.

Mia, Lainey, and Gabby came running after them, shouting. But they couldn't keep up with the fairy or the flying dog.

"Kate!" Coach Christy yelled.

Kate's attention snapped back to the field just as the kicker booted the ball.

At the same moment, Vidia crossed onto the field, flying through the middle of the game. Rascal was right behind her, bounding like a deer. For a second, the dog and the ball seemed almost to cross in the air.

Kate made a split-second decision.

She pushed off and felt the fairy dust lift her into the air. She heard the other players gasp as she sailed up, her arms open for the catch.

Kate tackled Rascal. She landed on the ground hard with the dog in her arms. The ball flew into the net behind her, just as the clock ran down.

Chapter 10

"I'm sorry you lost the game," Lainey said to Kate.

The four friends were sitting under a blossoming cherry tree in the park. Rascal sat with them. Lainey had a tight grip on his leash. But for once the dog wasn't trying to run away or chase anything.

"Thanks." Kate sighed. "Coach Christy will probably never let me play goalie again."

"She might," Mia said. "That was a

pretty amazing save—even if you didn't actually catch the ball."

"Yeah." Kate half smiled thinking about it. "It was awesome. But I think that's the last time I'll ever play with fairy dust—I mean, except in Never Land."

"At least we got Rascal back," Gabby added.

She reached over to scratch the dog's ears. Rascal yawned and put his head down in Lainey's lap.

"Looks like we finally wore him out," Mia said.

"You know, he's actually kind of sweet when he's like this," Lainey said. "Maybe I should dog-sit more often."

"Noooooooo!" all her friends said together.

Lainey laughed. "Just kidding." She

stood up. "I'd better get going. Rascal's
family is going to be home soon. I have to
get him back."

The other girls stood up, too. "Want
to go to Never Land after Lainey takes
Rascal home?" Mia asked. "Kate, you must
still have some fairy dust left. You can
show us some more fancy soccer moves!"

"Yes!" said Gabby.

"I'm in," said Lainey.

"Me too," said Kate. "But those soccer moves will have to wait. There's one more thing I have to do."

*

Vidia sat on a branch in the cherry tree, leaning against a soft pink blossom. She could hear Kate and her friends talking below her, but she didn't bother to listen. She just wanted to sit and be still for a moment. She felt tired to her bones.

Out beyond the park, she heard the rush of traffic. A siren wailed. The Clumsy world was not what Vidia had thought it would be. It was faster than Pixie Hollow, yes. But it was full of noise and dust and chaos. Vidia found herself thinking fondly of the soft, lavender-scented air, the drowsy bees, and even the sleepy pace of her home.

Maybe, she thought, it was better to be the fastest in a slow place than to be one of many fast things in a very fast place.

"Vidia!" Kate interrupted her thoughts. "Vidia, where are you?"

What does she want? Vidia thought with a scowl. She hunkered closer to the pillowy cherry blossom, hoping Kate would go away.

Kate's large freckled face appeared between the branches. "Oh! There you are. I was looking for you. . . ." She stopped and stared.

"What?" Vidia asked.

"Nothing," Kate said. "I just don't think I've ever seen you sitting still before."

Vidia shrugged.

"We're going to Pixie Hollow. Are you coming?" Kate asked, adding, "I'm ready to race you now."

"Race?" For the first time ever in her life, Vidia didn't feel like racing. But she was too proud to admit it. She stood, drawing herself up to her full five and a half inches. "What would I want to race you for?"

"But you said—"

"We both know you'd never win," Vidia went on. "I have better things to do than race Clumsies, my sweet."

Vidia rose from the branch and began to circle the cherry tree. Faster and faster

she flew, whipping up
a windstorm that tore
at the cherry blossoms.

Faster. Faster. Faster!

Smiling, Vidia blew the petals right off
the tree—just because she could.

Read this sneak peek of *Chasing Magic,*
the first book in a new series.

𝔇𝗂𝗌𝗇𝖾𝗒 · PIXAR

Merida

by Sudipta Bardhan-Quallen
illustrated by Gurihiru

The sun had barely risen, but Castle DunBroch was already alive with activity. Only one person was still in bed.

"Merida!" The queen's voice echoed through the halls. Merida pulled her pillow over her head. Anything to try to block out the sound. Her mother could be heard from anywhere in the castle—even around corners and through stone walls.

"Merida!" The voice was getting closer.

Now Merida heard footsteps approaching. "Ach," she muttered. "It's too early."

Without warning, the blankets were ripped away.

"Merida," said Queen Elinor, "how many times have I told you that a princess rises with the sun?"

"I don't know," Merida mumbled. "I don't think human beings have discovered a number that's high enough yet."

"A princess never mumbles," her mum added.

Merida opened her eyes just enough to see her mother standing over her. There she was, hair perfectly combed. Her mouth was a tight line. She arched a single eyebrow.

"I'm sorry, Mum—" Merida began.

But Elinor simply jumped into bed next to her daughter. She pulled the blankets over them both.

"If the princess is going to loll about in bed long after the sun is in the sky," she said, "then I think the queen is allowed to join her."

Merida smiled and threw an arm over her mother.

"Did you forget what today is?" Elinor asked.

Merida's eyebrows scrunched as she tried to remember. "Someone's arriving?" she asked.

"Yes, someone is arriving!" Elinor said. "Haven't you been paying attention?"

Merida bit her lip and looked away. She hadn't been following events in the kingdom very closely. After all, the Queen of DunBroch was responsible for treaties and truces. Merida was not the queen.

"Oh, Merida!" said Mum. She reached over and cupped her daughter's chin. She lifted her face until they were eye to eye. "I know this treaty doesn't seem as interesting to you as climbing or riding or shooting at things with that bow of yours. . . ."

"It's called archery, Mum."

"I *know* it's called archery, silly goose," Elinor said. "Treaties may not seem as interesting," she continued, "but they are important. I expect you, as Princess of DunBroch, to learn from this. That way you will know what to do when you are queen yourself."

"Fine, Mum," Merida mumbled.

"Did you practice your song?" Elinor asked.

Merida pulled the blankets up higher. Mum wanted her to be ready to sing a song for the guests. But singing was one of those princess skills that Merida would never master.

Mum sighed. "You *will* practice today?"

But Merida wasn't loving the thought of getting out of bed. "Just a bit longer?"

"No lolling about, Merida," Mum said. "A princess never lolls about." But when she rose from the bed, she tucked the blankets around her daughter. "A *wee* bit more," she whispered, and then straightened her skirts and crown. "Then get dressed and come to the games field. You can practice your song there."

Elinor turned to Merida's armoire. A wimple was hanging from one corner. Merida's heart plummeted. Mum hadn't made her wear that stupid thing since the Highland Games, when she had it wrapped around Merida's head and hair like a cloth prison. But today would be the first important day since the Games. Merida should have known that a "traditional" headdress would be a part of that.

Elinor lifted the wimple and fingered the white fabric. "Merida," she said. Her eyes locked with her daughter's. Merida held her breath. "Don't wear this ridiculous thing today, please?"

The games field was buzzing with people when Merida arrived. But Mum was nowhere to be found. Merida only saw her father, King Fergus, holding court.

"Everything must go well today," Fergus bellowed. Lords Dingwall, Macintosh, and MacGuffin, who had traveled from their own lands to help with the treaty, nodded solemnly.

"Elinor will kill me if anything goes wrong!"

"And a treaty would help our people prosper," Lord Dingwall added.

Fergus grinned sheepishly. "Yes, of course—that, too." When he spotted Merida, he whispered to her, "But keeping your mum happy is even more important!"

As Merida giggled, the games field grew silent.

The lords turned and bowed. Fergus smoothed his kilt. The triplets even hid the cakes they had stolen behind their backs. Only one person could command the people of DunBroch in this way. Mum had made her entrance.

"My people," Elinor began. "This is an historic day. The Lord of Cardonagh's ships will land today to discuss a treaty between our kingdoms. If we come to an agreement, the people of DunBroch will be able to trade freely with the people of Cardonagh. This will bring prosperity."

"Aye!" cried Fergus. He crossed the field to lead Elinor up to the dais. They clasped hands and stood side by side while the people cheered for their king and queen. Merida smiled. Her parents were so happy together. Their love was the cornerstone of the kingdom.

"Just as the clans DunBroch, Macintosh, MacGuffin, and Dingwall once united," Elinor continued, "now we ally with other friends." The queen looked over to Merida and held out her hand. Merida took a deep breath and walked to the dais. She held her head up like her mother. *Princesses walk with dignity,* Mum had said so many times. Merida wanted her to know that she *did* listen. Sometimes.

As Merida approached, Elinor took her hand. "Upon signing this treaty," she said, "DunBroch and Cardonagh will be allies. The future is most precious to us. My daughter, Merida, is your princess. This treaty is for her and for all our children."

"Hear, hear!" shouted Lord Dingwall. Others began to cheer as well. Elinor held up her hand for silence.

"To honor our hopes for the future, Lord Braden is bringing a member of his family, his heir, to DunBroch."

Merida's head snapped up. An heir? She didn't remember anyone mentioning any heirs. Suddenly, she wished she *had* paid more attention to the preparations.

Merida's heart began to pound. What was her mother about to say?

"If we are successful," Elinor said, "then we will celebrate a lifelong bond between DunBroch and Cardonagh."

Lifelong bond? Merida thought her parents had given up on the idea of arranging a marriage between her and some lord's son. But an heir and a lifelong bond? Marriage might be back on the table.

No, Mum wouldn't do that, she thought. But then the crowd erupted in cheers. Elinor and Fergus grasped Merida's hands and raised them into the air in celebration. *This is lucky,* Merida thought. *If I faint, they'll be holding me up.*

As soon as the cheering died down, Merida

tried to pull Mum aside. But Elinor was busy discussing the banquet with Maudie. Merida knew that once Mum started talking about haggis, it would be a long time before she was done.

Merida sighed and looked for her father instead. But Fergus had gone to meet the ships from Cardonagh. There was no one to ask about the heir and why he was coming.

"Mum and Dad would never arrange another marriage," Merida whispered. Why did it sound like she was trying to convince herself?

Merida glanced at her mother again.

"Some people like a baked haggis," Elinor said, "but I prefer a boiled haggis." Maudie nodded solemnly.

There was no way to get any answers out of

Mum now. Merida needed some time to think.

She quietly backed away from the hulla-balloo. When she was out of sight, she ran back to the castle and to her room.

In a few minutes, she was headed toward her horse with her bow in hand.

"I need some time alone, Angus," Merida said when she reached the stable. "Let's go for a ride."

Soon Angus and Merida were flying through the Highlands. The familiar twang of the bowstring resounded as Merida fired shot after shot. When the princess was riding with a bow, she felt as free as the wind. In no time, she almost forgot about the Lord of Cardonagh.

Up ahead, hidden in the high branches of a tree, Merida spied a ripe, juicy apple. She

brought Angus to a halt. "I'll get that down for you, Angus. Won't that be yummy?"

It was a difficult shot to make, almost straight overhead. But if she hit the stem of the apple, it would fall at Angus's feet, making it easy for him to snack on.

Merida drew her bow. Before she released the string, an arrow flew toward the apple. It sliced the stem perfectly. The apple plopped to the ground.

"What was that?" Still holding her arrow in place, Merida turned to look over her shoulder.

Behind her, on horseback, was a strange girl holding a longbow.

The girl asked, "Did I take your target?"